For my mommy, Ann
—A. K. R.

For Lea-Marie and Livia
—L. P.

Text copyright © 2010 by Amy Krouse Rosenthal
Illustrations copyright © 2010 by LeUyen Pham

Published by Bloomsbury U.S.A. Children's Books
175 Fifth Avenue, New York, New York 10010

Library of Congress Cataloging-in-Publication Data
Rosenthal, Amy Krouse.
Bedtime for Mommy / by Amy Krouse Rosenthal;
illustrated by LeUyen Pham.—1st U.S. ed.
p. cm.
Summary: In a reversal of the classic bedtime story, a child helps her mommy
get ready for bed, enduring pleas for one more book, five more minutes
of play time, and a glass of water before the lights go out.
ISBN 978-1-59990-341-5 (hardcover) · ISBN 978-1-59990-465-8 (reinforced)
[1. Bedtime—Fiction. 2. Mothers and daughters—Fiction. 3. Humorous stories.]
I. Pham, LeUyen, ill. II. Title.
PZ7.R719445Be 2010   [E]—dc22   2009018205

Art created with watercolor and India ink on hot press paper
Typeset in Nueva
Book design by Donna Mark

First U.S. Edition April 2010
Printed in China by Printplus Limited, Shenzhen, Guangdong
2 4 6 8 10 9 7 5 3 1 (hardcover)
2 4 6 8 10 9 7 5 3 1 (reinforced)

Bedtime for Mommy

Amy Krouse Rosenthal

illustrated by
LeUyen Pham

BLOOMSBURY

NEW YORK BERLIN LONDON

Time for bed, Mommy!

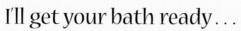

I'll get your bath ready...

Here are your bath toys.

Did you brush your teeth?

Yep.

A nice long time?

Yep.

Good mommy.

Perfect.

Thank you.

Love you.

Love you more.

A little open, please.

A little more.

Little more.

That's good.

Good night!

Okay. One down, one to go.